DATE DUE

Please Return To:
Grace Christian School Library
325 M-140
Watervliet, MI 49098
616-463-5545

JANE EYRE
By Charlotte Brontë

Adapted by Diana Stewart
Illustrated by Charles Shaw

RSVP
RAINTREE
STECK-VAUGHN
PUBLISHERS
The Steck-Vaughn Company

Austin, Texas

Library of Congress Number: 80-14426

Library of Congress Cataloging-in-Publication Data

Stewart, Diana.
 Jane Eyre.

 (Raintree short classics)
 SUMMARY: Retells in simple language the events leading up to and following young Jane's arrival at Thornfield Hall, a country estate owned by the mysterious, Mr. Rochester.
 I. Shaw, Charlie. 2. Bronte, Charlotte, 1816-1855. Jane Eyre. III. Title. IV. Series.
 PZ7.S84878Jan   [Fic.]   80-14426

ISBN 0-8172-1661-8 hardcover library binding

ISBN 0-8114-6830-5 softcover binding

13 14 15 16 17 18   99 98 97 96 95 94

CONTENTS

THORNFIELD HALL

1

"We're nearly to Thornfield Hall now, Miss Eyre," the driver called over his shoulder as he opened the iron gate. Slowly the coach climbed the narrow lane toward the huge gray stone house. Through the mist of the black October night, I had my first look at Thornfield — and I shivered from nervousness. It is a frightening thing to be friendless and all alone in the world. I was shy about meeting strangers, and as I looked at the house, I wondered what my life would be like there.

A single candle burned in the window to welcome me. All the rest was dark. My heart pounded as we stopped at the front door.

Dear reader, what shall I tell you about myself so you will understand how I felt as I started on the biggest adventure of my life? First, let me explain that I had come to Thornfield as a governess. I had to earn my living without help from anyone, because I was an orphan. My parents died while I was still a baby, and I was put in the care of an aunt.

But my Aunt Reed was a hard, unfeeling woman — except where her own children were concerned. Perhaps if my parents had left me with a fortune, she might have welcomed me to her house. Or perhaps if I had been a pretty, lively child, my aunt might have loved me. But I was neither pretty nor rich — and she despised me. My two cousins — Georgiana and Eliza — for the most part ignored me. Their older brother John, however, took great pleasure in tormenting me. He teased and bullied me, not once or twice a week, but continually.

The crisis in my life came when I was ten. One day I sat reading. Books were my only comfort, and with a book on my lap, hiding behind the curtains of the window seat, I was happy. But suddenly John called me. I trembled at the idea of his opening the curtains and dragging me from my place, so I went to him. I knew that soon he would hit me, and I dreaded it as always. Then without warning he struck.

"That's for being rude and sneaking off behind the drapes," he said. "What were you doing?"

"I was reading," I replied.

"Show me the book!" I fetched the book and handed it over to him. "You have no business taking our books," he yelled. "Your father left you no money. You ought to be begging in the streets, not living with gentlemen's children!" And he threw the book at me. I tried to duck, but I wasn't quick enough. It hit me and I fell back, hitting my head on the door. Blood poured out of the cut.

"You wicked, wicked boy!" I cried. "You are like a murderer! You are like a slave-driver!"

"What? Eliza, Georgiana, did you hear? Did you hear what she said? Won't I tell Mama! But first . . . "

And he flew at me. Blood ran down my face from the cut, and I was afraid. I fought him like a wild thing and he bellowed and called for help. My aunt soon came followed by the servants. "Take her away!" she said. "Take her upstairs and lock her in the red room!"

"For shame, Miss Eyre!" the maid said as she led me up the stairs. "For shame — striking your master like that!"

"Master! How is he my master? Am I a servant?"

"No, you are less than a servant. You are nothing. If it wasn't for Mrs. Reed's kindness, you would be in a poorhouse. Now, sit there on that stool and think about your wickedness."

Unjust! Unjust! my heart cried. I only tried to please. I only wanted their love and respect, but they hated me.

And from that day on my aunt would not speak to me. She refused to have me in her house any longer, and within a few weeks, she had arranged for me to go to Lowood, a school for orphans. There I stayed for eight years. Until this morning when I began my journey to Thornfield Hall, I had never left Lowood.

Do you understand, reader, why I had both hopes and fears? I hoped to find a home and friends at Thornfield, but I knew nothing of the place or its people. And I trembled as I knocked on the huge wooden doors.

"Miss Eyre?" asked the maid who answered. "Follow me, please. Mrs. Fairfax is waiting for you."

She led me to a small sitting room. A fire burned brightly in the grate. There sat Mrs. Fairfax, an elderly lady dressed in a black silk dress and white apron.

"You are Jane Eyre?" she asked pleasantly. "Come in, my dear. You must be frozen. I will ring for tea."

I had not expected such kindness, and my heart was warmed. Mrs. Fairfax was not the stiff, formal matron I had feared, and with her friendly smile and idle chatter, my tense nerves gradually relaxed.

"Adela is asleep, but you shall meet her tomorrow," she said when tea had been served.

"Adela is my student?" I asked. "She is your daughter?"

"My daughter? Oh, dear me, no. I am the housekeeper of Thornfield Hall. Adela is the ward of Mr. Rochester — the master here."

"Mr. Rochester?" Do not wonder at my surprise, dear reader. This was the first I had heard of the gentleman. I had been hired by Mrs. Fairfax.

"Why, yes," the lady said. "He is away now. In fact, he seldom lives with us. He is a great gentleman and spends most of his time in London or traveling."

"And I am to teach his ward?"

"That's right. He brought Adela here from Paris not long ago and put her in my care."

The clock struck midnight, and Mrs. Fairfax rose to her

feet. "But come, Miss Eyre. It is late, and I am sure you are tired. I will show you to your room."

The room was on the second floor. It was small and comfortable, and a fire was burning to warm it. For me, this was indeed a luxury.

"Sleep well, Miss Eyre," Mrs. Fairfax said. "Tomorrow I will show you the house, and you can begin your lessons with Adela. We live very quietly here, my dear, but I hope you will be happy."

The next day I dressed with my usual neatness. Although I was plain, I always wanted to look my best. Sometimes I wished I was prettier. I wished to have rosy cheeks, a straight nose, and a small cherry mouth. I desired to be tall and stately with a fine figure. I wanted to be able to laugh and be merry. Instead I was little and pale and shy. I hoped Adela, my pupil, would at least like me.

I found her with Mrs. Fairfax in the small sitting room. Adela was a pretty child of about seven or eight. She had large hazel eyes and curly hair that fell nearly to her waist. When I spoke to her in French, her eyes brightened and soon we were chattering happily away.

The library had been set aside for our studies. Adela did not complain about doing her lessons, but she was not a hard worker and would have much rather be allowed to run free. In the days that followed, however, we got along well, and I was happy for the most part.

Adela was a good, cheerful child. Mrs. Fairfax treated me with great kindness, and I soon became fond of them both.

For three months my life followed a single pattern. I taught Adela her lessons each morning. In the afternoon I read or drew in my sketch book. If the weather was good, I walked through the orchards and fields around Thornfield. In the evenings I ate with Mrs. Fairfax in the small sitting room. We then sat by the fire and talked. But though she was a good, kind woman, we had little in common. And I found the evenings very dull.

Once I tried to ask her questions about Mr. Rochester, but she could tell me little about him. He was a distant cousin of hers and a good, fair master, she said. He had not owned Thornfield long, however. When his father died, his older brother had inherited the estate. Then a few years before, his brother had also died, and now Mr. Edward Rochester was master.

There were several servants in the house, but one was a mystery to me. Her name was Grace Poole. I first heard of her when Mrs. Fairfax was showing me through the house. We were in a part of the second floor that was seldom used. From above us I heard the sound of a strange laugh — long and low and deep.

"Does Thornfield Hall have a ghost?" I asked.

"No, not that I know of," Mrs. Fairfax replied. "Oh, you mean the laughter! That is only Grace Poole. She has rooms on the floor above this. Mr. Rochester hires her to do the sewing."

I was curious about Grace Poole, but I only saw her a few times. She was an odd woman of about thirty-five — large, plain, and unsmiling. She spoke little to anyone. She would come to the kitchen each day, take a tray of food, and return to the third floor.

And so October, November, and December passed quietly away. Dear reader, I have told you about my new home. Will you think I was ungrateful if I tell you I grew bored and restless? But I did. In January, however, my life changed.

Near the end of the month, Adela caught a cold and had to stay in bed. My day was free. I was tired of sitting in the house, and I offered to walk the two miles into the village of Hay to mail a letter for Mrs. Fairfax.

The air was cold and I walked fast until I got warm. The lonely road twisted and turned over the hills. Halfway up one hill, I stopped beside a gate to get my breath. Suddenly, from up the path I heard the sound of a horse. The road was narrow, so I stayed on the gate as the horse came nearer and nearer. Then, over the hill bounded a large black and white dog. He was quickly followed by the horse and rider. The three passed me by without a glance, and I

11

started on my way again. But I had only gone a few steps when I heard the horse groan and the dog begin to bark.

"What to do now?" a man's voice said.

I turned and saw that the horse had slipped on a patch of ice, and the rider was on the ground.

"Are you injured, sir?" I asked, hurrying back. I think the man was swearing, and he did not answer me. "Can I help you?" I asked again.

"Stand aside!" he ordered. He got first to his knees and then to his feet. "Down Pilot!" he said to the dog barking at his heels.

"If you are hurt and want help," I offered, "I will bring someone from Hay or Thornfield Hall."

"Don't bother. I shall be all right," he answered curtly. But he took a step and groaned.

The day was dim, but I could see his face clearly. It was a stern face with heavy eyebrows and dark eyes now filled with anger. He was not young — perhaps thirty-five or forty. If he had been young and handsome, I might have left him and gone on my way. But this rough, frowning stranger did not make me shy or nervous.

"I cannot leave you like this, sir," I said. "Not until I am sure you are all right."

He looked at me now for the first time. "You should be home yourself," he said. "Where do you come from?"

"From over there," I answered, pointing toward Thornfield.

"Whose house is it?"

"Mr. Rochester's."

"Do you know Mr. Rochester?"

"No, I have never seen him."

"You are a servant at the hall, of course. You are — " He stopped and looked at my simple black cloak and black hat.

"I am the governess."

"Of course! The governess. I had forgotten. Well, come then, little governess, and be useful. You shall be my crutch. I beg your pardon, but I must lean on you."

I stood by him, and he placed his hand on my shoulder. With my help, he made his way back to his horse. Once there, he was able to mount and I handed him his whip from the ground.

"Thank you," was all he said — and he was gone.

Once more I was on my way, but the stranger had brought something new to the dull day. My thoughts kept returning to his face — dark and strong and stern.

When I returned home an hour later, I could hear voices coming from the drawing room. I hurried to the sitting room to find Mrs. Fairfax. It was empty except for a great black and white dog that lay by the fire.

"Pilot?" I called, and the dog raised his head and came to sniff at me. I rang the bell for a servant. "Whose dog is this?" I asked when she entered.

"It belongs to the master," she answered. "He just arrived, but he had an accident. He sprained his ankle on the road. The doctor is with him now."

I now knew who the stranger was that I had met. Mr. Rochester had come home.

MR. ROCHESTER

2

I did not see the master that night. But the next evening Adela and I were asked to go to him in the drawing room.

"Here is Miss Eyre," Mrs. Fairfax said.

"Sit down, Miss Eyre," he ordered. He did not even look at me. He continued to frown into the fire — and I was glad. I would not have known what to do if he had been smiling and polite, but his frown did not demand anything of me. "Mrs. Fairfax, ring for some tea," he added curtly.

Mr. Rochester did not speak again until after tea had been served. Then he turned to look at me with his dark, piercing black eyes.

"How long have you lived here, Miss Eyre?"

"Three months, sir."

"And where did you come from?"

"From Lowood School — "

"Ah, a charity school," he interrupted. "How long were you there?"

"Eight years, sir. Six years as a student and two as a teacher."

"You survived eight years in a place like that? You must be stronger than you look. Have you no family?"

"None that will claim me, sir."

"Who recommended you to come here?"

"I advertised in the paper, and Mrs. Fairfax answered my advertisement."

"Did they treat you well at Lowood?"

"Sir, it was a school for orphans. The people there did not starve us or beat us, but it was cold and we had little to eat. Their one purpose was to make us humble and hard-working."

On and on his questions went. Did I read? Did I play the piano? Did I draw? I answered all these as honestly as I could. Finally, he waved me away.

"It is nine o'clock. Take Adela to bed."

Mr. Rochester did not send for me again for several days. He was busy with the farmers who worked his land. At first, they came to the hall. Then when his ankle was better, he went out riding each day. Now and then I would pass him in the hall, but he hardly noticed me. At last, over a week later, he sent for me once more.

For several minutes after I joined him in the drawing room, he sat and stared into the fire. This gave me a chance to study him. Suddenly, however, he turned and caught my eye on him.

"You look at me, Miss Eyre," he said. "Do you think I am handsome?"

"No, sir," I said before I realized what I was saying.

"My word!" he exclaimed. "You are very blunt!"

"I beg your pardon, sir. I spoke too quickly. I should have said that looks are not important."

"Nonsense! Say what you like to me. You are small and plain, but you are honest. I sent for you because I feel like talking to someone tonight. Adela has nothing of interest to say and Mrs. Fairfax is not much better. But you, I think, are different. Tell me, what goes on behind that quiet, solemn face of yours?"

For nearly an hour he talked. He spoke of his travels. He talked of sin and of trying to live a better life. It was an odd conversation to have with a stranger, but I listened to him with interest.

"Are you afraid of me because I am old and ugly?" he asked at last.

"No, sir."

"Yet you sit there so quietly. Do you never laugh? No, I

see that you do not. Did they teach you not to laugh at Lowood? Was laughing a sin? Did they teach you that life is a serious business, and the only happiness a person can hope for is in heaven?"

"Yes, sir," I answered simply.

"And yet you let Adela laugh."

"She is a happy child, sir. She is grateful to you for bringing her to Thornfield."

"And you wonder why I brought her here. You know I am not married, but you wonder if she is my child. Well, someday I will tell you about her."

And he did tell me about Adela a few days later. She was the daughter of a French singer he had known in Paris. She was not his daughter, but when her mother died, he brought her to England to raise her. Mr. Rochester might be grim and stern and sometimes rude, but he had a kind heart. I was sure that someone or something had made him very bitter, and I knew his life had not been easy.

From then on, he sent for me often. Dear reader, will you think I am bragging if I say that he enjoyed my company? I knew I gave him pleasure and seemed to have the power to make him happy.

Weeks passed. His manner with me now was friendly and casual. Sometimes I felt that he was more my friend or relative than my master. In his company I was never bored, and in his home my body grew strong and healthy.

And was Mr. Rochester still ugly in my eyes? No, gentle reader. His face became the one I liked to see best. When he was in the room, his presence was more cheerful to me than the brightest fire. I had not forgotten his faults, how-ever. He was proud and harsh with others — but never with me. Often he was moody and would sit staring into the fire. I knew his memories gave him pain, and often his thoughts would bring the dark, bitter look to his face.

I was happy at Thornfield Hall, but my master hated the house. He told me so often, and I wondered if it did indeed have a ghost that haunted him.

One night I awoke suddenly. Some noise had interrupted my sleep. Then, from out in the hall, I heard the strange, low, deep laugh I had heard before. Was Grace Poole wandering through the house in the middle of the night?

"Who's there?" I called.

There was no answer, but I heard a cry and a moan. Quickly I slipped into my clothes and opened the door to the hall. No one was in sight. But as I turned to go back into my room, I smelled smoke coming from down the hall. The door to Mr. Rochester's room creaked open, and smoke poured from the room. In an instant I was there. Flames were leaping up the curtains around the bed where Mr. Rochester lay asleep.

"Wake up!" I cried. I shook him, but he only moaned.

I could not wait a minute. The sheets were already starting to burn. I grabbed a pitcher of water from the table nearby and threw it over the bed and my sleeping master. I ran to my own room for another pitcher. I threw that on the flames also. Tearing at the curtains, I stamped out the fire. At last all was dark. From the bed, I heard Mr. Rochester stir.

"What the — " he exclaimed. "Is there a flood?"

"No, sir," I answered. "There has been a fire, but it is out now. Just a minute, and I will get a candle."

"Jane Eyre! Is that you? What on earth is going on?"

By the time I returned with the candle, he was up and dressed in his robe. Briefly I told him what had happened.

"Shall I call someone for help?" I asked.

"No," he said sharply. "Here, put your shawl around you, and sit here. Don't move until I come back."

I heard his footsteps echo down the hall and then climb the steps to the third floor. I grew cold and tired waiting, but finally he returned.

"Was it Grace Poole?" I asked. "She is an odd woman. I have heard her laughing before."

"Yes," he said. "It was Grace Poole — you have guessed it. Can I trust you, Jane, to say nothing of what happened tonight?"

"You know you can, sir. But why? The woman is dangerous."

"You must trust me, Jane, even as I trust you. Say nothing. I will tell Mrs. Fairfax that I fell asleep with a candle burning and the curtains caught fire."

"Very well. Good night, sir."

"What? You would go — just like that? You save my life. You save me from a terrible death, and you would just leave me?"

"I am tired, sir," I answered quietly.

"Yes, perhaps you had better go, but at least shake hands."

I gave him my hand and he held it between his own. "I knew you would do me good, Jane. Your face, your smile — they did not bring me joy for nothing."

He wanted to say more. I saw the words tremble on his lips, but he was silent. His eyes, however, spoke for him. They looked at me in a way that made my heart pound.

"Go, Jane. You must go! But Jane — I thank you!"

THE HOUSE PARTY

3

I longed to see Mr. Rochester the next morning. I wanted to hear his voice, but at the same time, I was afraid. When morning came, however, my feelings did not matter. My master was gone.

"Has he returned to London?" I asked Mrs. Fairfax.

"No," she replied. "He is visiting some friends in the neighborhood. He will be gone a week or two."

I heard the answer, and I could be happy again. He had not gone away from me — out of my life.

"He is visiting Miss Ingram," Mrs. Fairfax continued. "Such a beautiful lady. She comes from a good family and is so talented. He visits her whenever he is in England. I have thought for a long time that he would marry her."

Her words gave me such pain! Fool! I told myself. Why should you think that you are something special to Mr. Rochester? Just because you saved his life and he looked at you — oh, in such a way! He loves a young, beautiful woman. Do not wish for what can never be yours.

I had an opportunity to see Blanche Ingram for myself ten days later. Mr. Rochester sent word that he was bringing his friends home with him. All the best bedrooms must be prepared, he ordered. The company, twelve in all, would stay for some time.

When they arrived, I saw Miss Ingram riding beside Mr. Rochester. She was just as Mrs. Fairfax described her — a tall, well-built lady, with black hair and black, flashing eyes. I watched her turn and laugh up into my master's face.

Oh, dear reader, my heart ached. My face grew pale. I trembled. I had not meant to fall in love with Mr. Rochester. He had made me love him without even trying!

The next week was agony to me. Each evening I brought Adela down to sit with the company in the drawing room. Never did Mr. Rochester look at me or speak to me. From a corner, I silently watched him with his lady and friends. They laughed and joked and talked and played games. Mr. Rochester and Miss Ingram sang together. He had a beautiful, deep, rich voice. It was both a joy and a pain to hear him.

I listened to Miss Ingram's conversation, and it hurt me to think he could love a woman like her. She was petty and mean. She laughed at the servants and gossiped unkindly.

He is not like that, I thought. They have nothing in common! He cannot marry her! While I lived, I could not put hope out of my heart. While I breathed, I had to love him.

Only once in those long days did he speak to me. He stopped me one evening in the hallway as I was slipping away to my room.

"What have you been doing, Jane, while I have been busy?" he asked.

"Nothing, sir."

"Yet you are pale and unhappy. Tell me what is the matter," he demanded.

"Nothing, sir."

"And I say something is the matter. My words have made you cry. A tear has fallen from your eye."

"Please, sir. Let me go to bed."

"All right. Go if you must! Good night, my—" He stopped, bit his lip, and left me.

One day after nearly two weeks, Mr. Rochester left his guests for the day on business. We were all restless without him, but just before evening tea, a stranger arrived and relieved the boredom of the guests. The man had just come from Jamaica, he said, and he had business with Mr. Rochester.

I met my master with the news when he arrived home.

"Sir," I said. "There is a man here to see you. A Mr. Mason from Jamaica. He is in the drawing room."

"Mason! The West Indies!" His hand shook and his face grew pale.

"Are you ill, sir?" I asked.

"Jane! This is a blow!" And he staggered.

"Here, sir. Lean on me."

I helped him sit down and brought him a glass of wine. Slowly the color came back into his face as he drank.

"Can I help you, sir?" I asked. "I'd give you my life."

"I don't ask that of you, Jane. But go into the drawing room. Tell Mason I am here and want to see him. Don't let the others hear you. Then bring him back here to me."

I did as he asked and then went to my room. I did not go back down that night. I lay on my bed, but I could not sleep. It was after three o'clock that a scream rang through the house, and I heard a voice above me call for help:

"Rochester! Rochester! For God's sake, come!"

The whole house was awakened by the scream. By the time I put on my clothes, my master had arrived in the hall outside.

"It was just a servant," he explained to his guests. "She had a nightmare. Please, go back to your beds."

All was quiet for several minutes. I stood by my door waiting — not sure what I waited for. But a moment later I heard Mr. Rochester's voice.

"Jane? Are you awake? I need your help."

Quickly I opened the door, and my master took me by the hand. "Come with me," he said, and he led me up the stairs to the floor above, to Grace Poole's room.

The sight that met my eyes was terrible. There in a chair lay Mr. Mason. His arm was bleeding and he had fainted. There was no sign of Grace Poole.

"Stay here with him," Mr. Rochester said. "I am going for the doctor."

I sat alone with the injured man. A single candle lighted the room. I dreaded the thought that Grace Poole might

suddenly appear, but I kept watch until the doctor arrived.

"Good God!" the doctor cried when he saw the wound. "This was not done just with a knife. There are teeth marks here."

"She bit me!" Mason murmured. "Oh, it was terrible! She sucked the blood. She said she would drain my heart."

"Be quiet, Richard," Mr. Rochester said. "Do not repeat it. You must put it out of your mind and forget it. I have a carriage waiting outside. You will leave tonight."

"Yes," Mason said weakly. "But let her be taken care of. Treat her tenderly—." And he burst into tears.

"I do my best. I always have and I always will."

I followed my master and the doctor as they helped Mason to a waiting carriage.

"This has been a strange night, Jane," Mr. Rochester said when the others had gone.

"Yes, sir."

"Come, Jane. Walk in the orchard with me. We will sit at the end of the garden and talk."

Willingly I followed him and sat beside him on a bench.

"What would you do, Jane," he said, "if you had made a terrible mistake. I don't say committed a crime — just made a mistake. Would you have to pay for it the rest of your life?"

"It would be in God's hands, sir," I answered quietly.

"Jane, you have seen me with Miss Ingram. If I married her, would she bring me the happiness and peace I seek?"

"I cannot say, sir."

"But isn't she beautiful and talented? Isn't she everything that a man could desire? Jane, the night before I am married, will you promise to sit with me and keep me company?"

"Yes, sir," I said. "I will if you will promise me that before you bring a bride home to Thornfield, I can be gone."

"You want to leave me, Jane?"

"I think I must, sir."

"And the thought makes you sad. I see tears in your eyes. Your little hands are trembling. We will talk again, Jane. Now you are cold and tired. You must go in."

I left him with an aching heart.

Several weeks passed. The house party broke up and the guests left. Nothing more was said of Mr. Rochester's coming marriage. Each night he called me to the drawing room with Adela. But the sadder I grew, the happier he became. Never had he been kinder to me — and never had I loved him so well.

June came and the weather was warm. One evening I walked out into the orchard. As I neared the end of the garden, I smelled the smoke of a cigar. I knew that Mr. Rochester was out walking also.

I meant to slip quietly away, but he called out to me. "Jane, come here — here by the chestnut tree. Come and sit."

Silently I sat by his side, my hands in my lap.

"What would you say, Jane, if I told you that I was going to bring a bride to Thornfield?"

"I would say it was time for me to leave, sir."

I turned my head so that he could not see my tears.

"You want to leave me, then? I could send you to friends in Ireland, Jane."

"It is a long way away — Ireland."

"Yes, it is a long way away," he continued. "And Jane, I have the strangest feeling when you are near me like this. I feel that there is a string tied tightly under my left rib. It is tied to a rib in your own little body. I believe that if you go away, the string will snap, and I will bleed inside."

A sob escaped my lips.

"You are crying? Why? Because you will be leaving?"

The pain of my love for him overcame me. I could no longer sit and listen to him. "I cry because I must leave Thornfield. Because I must leave you! Do you think because I am poor and plain and small that I have no heart? You are wrong! If God had made me rich and beautiful, I

would make it as hard for you to let me go as it is for me to leave! I do not speak to you as a servant. I speak to you as your equal — as we are!"

"Yes! Equal — as we are!" he repeated, and he put his arms around me and held me close, his lips on mine.

"Let me go, let me go!" I cried.

"Where? Away from me? Never, my Jane. Now stop struggling like a little bird. Stay with me."

"I can't stay with you!"

"Not even if I ask you to stay with me as my bride?"

"You have chosen another bride — Miss Ingram!"

"Do you doubt me, Jane?"

"Yes!"

"Am I a liar, then! I shall convince you. I have no love for Miss Ingram, and she has no love for me. She only loves my name and fortune. I would not — could not — marry her. I will have you or no one. Say you will marry me, Jane. Say it quickly. You torture me with your silence! Say Edward — call me by my name — Edward, I will marry you. I will be yours."

"Do you mean it, sir? Do you truly love me? Do you want me for your wife?"

"I do. I swear it!"

"Then, sir, I will marry you."

"Come to me, then. Come to me now!"

He took me into his arms and his lips met mine. Then he pressed his cheek against my hair, looking up to heaven. "God forgive me!" I heard him say. "God forgive me, but I have her, and I will not let her go!"

A spot of rain fell on my face, and then it seemed as if the heavens opened. The rain fell in sheets. The thunder and lightning sounded through the trees.

"Come, Jane. We must go in."

Together we ran towards the house. Behind us I heard a crash. Over my shoulder I looked to the chestnut tree where we had stood. There it lay, half of its huge branches on the ground. The lightning had struck it and split it half away.

THE WEDDING

4

The month before our wedding passed quickly. I refused to give up teaching Adela. Mr. Rochester wanted to shower me with fine dresses and jewels, but I would not let him. I treated him as I had always done. I sat with him only in the evenings. I held him at arms' length until it nearly drove him mad. Often I made him cross, and he called me rude names. But I knew that he secretly enjoyed the game we played.

"Tease me now," he said one night, "because in a few short days, you will be mine. And then you will not escape me!"

During the month, Mr. Rochester became my whole world. No, more than my world. He was my hope of heaven and the promise of every joy.

The day before we were to be married, I stood in my room. Around me were my trunks — all packed and ready to go. We were to be wed at eight the next morning. Then we would leave Thornfield for London, Rome, and Paris.

Mr. Rochester had gone out very early that morning to finish some business. Evening came, and still he did not return. I could no longer sit still and wait for him, so I started walking to meet him. At last he came. He saw me, and I ran to him. For once I let him hold and kiss me.

"What is it, Jane? You are trembling."

"I will tell you later, sir. After you have eaten."

It was late when we left the table and sat in the drawing room. He was in the chair by the fire, and I sat on a stool by his knee.

"Now, tell me, Jane. What is troubling you? You are nervous. Are you frightened of being my wife?"

"No, sir. I long to be your wife. I think it is a glorious thing to have the hope of living with you, Edward. Because I love you."

"Do you, Jane? Do you love me?"

"I do, sir. I love you with all my heart."

"You frighten me, Jane. You say it so seriously — with such faith and trust — but a little sadly. I would rather you tease me than be sad. Tell me what troubles you."

"Sir, something happened last night. I was awakened from my sleep by a candle on my dressing table. Someone was in the room. It was not Mrs. Fairfax or any of the servants or even the strange Grace Poole. It was someone I had never seen — a woman, sir. She was tall, dark, and very large. Her hair was long, black, and tangled. Her eyes were red and swollen. Her face was ghastly — purple and dark." I shuddered and moved nearer his knee.

"Did she come near you, Jane?"

"No, sir. She went to the cupboard where my wedding dress and veil hung. She took my veil from its place and put it on her head. Then with a cry, she tore it off her head and trampled it to the ground."

I could feel that Edward's body was tense, but he answered me calmly. "It was just a dream, Jane. You were having a nightmare."

"I thought so myself until this morning. There on the floor was my veil. It had been torn into pieces."

I felt him shudder, and he flung his arms around me. "Thank God!" he cried. "Thank God no harm came to you." He was quiet for a moment before he spoke again. Then he said slowly: "I will explain it, Jane. It was Grace Poole. You were only half awake and did not recognize her. She is a strange woman, but don't let her frighten you."

I thought about what he said. It did not seem possible that the woman I saw was Grace Poole. But I could see no other answer to the puzzle.

"And how is my Jane now?" he asked gently.

"The night is peaceful, sir; and so am I."

"Then to bed, my Jane. You will not dream of unhappiness tonight. You will dream of happy love and wedded bliss."

Half of his words were true. I did not dream of unhappiness. But I did not dream of joy either. In fact, I did not dream at all — because I did not sleep.

At seven the maid came to help me dress. For a veil I wore a plain square of cloth.

"Jane!" called a beloved voice from downstairs. "You take so long. My brain is on fire!" And I hurried down to my master.

He led me outside, and together we walked to the church near the front gate. Mr. Wood, the priest, was waiting. There were to be no bridesmaids, no relatives, no friends — only Edward and I. We took our places at the altar. I heard a step behind me and glanced over my shoulder. At the back of the chapel in the shadows stood two men.

The service began. Before we took our final vows, the priest came a step forward and said: "If anyone knows just cause why these two cannot lawfully be joined together in marriage, speak now!" He paused as is the custom, and then continued. "Wilt thou have this woman for thy wedded wife—"

"Stop!" a strange voice interrupted from behind us. "The marriage cannot go on. I declare a just cause!"

Mr. Wood looked up at the speaker and stood silent. Edward trembled and then said firmly: "Proceed, Mr. Wood!"

"I cannot proceed," replied the priest. "I must hear this man. Speak, sir, and tell us why they cannot be wed."

"The reason is simple! Mr. Rochester has a wife living now."

I looked at Edward, and he held me tight against him as he asked the stranger, "You say I have a wife already?"

"Not I, sir, but this gentleman. Mr. Mason, come forward."

I felt a spasm of fury tremble through Edward's body.

"Speak, Mr. Mason," said the priest.

"Sir, Mr. Rochester's wife is still living. I am her brother, and I saw her a few weeks ago — at Thornfield Hall."

"I have never heard of a Mrs. Rochester at Thornfield," Mr. Wood replied.

"No, by God!" my master said through clenched teeth. "I took care that no one should hear of her. Bigamy is an ugly word, Wood, but I meant to become a bigamist. Close your book. There will be no wedding today. Come with me — all of you. I will show you my wife!"

He took me by the arm and dragged me down the aisle, out of the church, and into the house. The three men followed behind us. Up, up we went — up to the third floor, to Grace Poole's rooms. In the corner a woman — no, an animal — ran back and forth. It crouched on all fours and growled and snarled.

"Be careful, sir!" Mrs. Poole said. "She sees you!"

"Behold, you see my wife!" he said to us. "My father and hers planned our marriage, even though they both knew she came from a family of idiots and madmen. Her mother was both a drunkard and insane. I did not know this until after we were married. I was tricked by my own father and yours, Mason. Oh, she was sane enough in the beginning to fool me. But soon her madness was evident. She drank and went with other men. Her temper became more and more violent until she was as you see her now."

Suddenly the creature stood and bellowed. I recognized the woman who had come to my room. Then, without warning, she sprang at her husband. Quickly he put me behind her. She caught him around the throat and sank her teeth into his cheek. She was a big woman, almost as big as Edward. He did not strike her. He only struggled with her until he had her arms behind her back. Mrs. Poole gave him a rope, and he tied her to a chair.

"This is my wife," he repeated. "For the last fifteen years, this is the love she has given me. Do you wonder that I kept her here in secret to hide my shame? Do you wonder that I wanted to forget her existence and marry this

quiet, young girl? But the law says she is mad, and I cannot divorce her. So I am left to live a life of misery, loneliness, and regret. Judge me for what I tried to do today if you dare! Now, off with you. I must lock up my prize!"

Alone in my room, I bolted the door and took off my wedding dress. I was too tired and weak to cry. My hopes were all dead. For hours I lay on my bed. What was I going to do? There was only one answer: I had to leave — leave Thornfield.

My head was dizzy as I went to the door. I opened it and fell, but not on the floor. Mr. Rochester sat in a chair across the doorway.

"You have come out at last," he said. "But you do not cry. Your face is white, and your eyes are dull, but I see no trace of tears. I suppose, then, your heart is weeping blood. What Jane? Not a word?" he asked when I was silent. "Jane, I never meant to hurt you! I only wanted to love you! Will you ever forgive me?"

Reader! I forgave him at that moment, on the spot. I did not forgive him in words but in my heart.

"Jane, you are silent. Forgive me! Say to me: 'I will be yours, Mr. Rochester.'"

"Mr. Rochester, I will *not* be yours."

"Jane, do you mean to go away?"

"I do."

I felt as if I were being torn apart. No one could ever love me better than he did. I could love no one better than him. My feelings called out to me: 'Stay with him — save him. Who in the world cares for *you*, or will be injured by what you do?' And yet the reply came: 'I care for myself. The more alone I am, the more I will respect myself.'

"Oh, Jane!" he cried. "This is wicked. It would not be a sin to love me."

"It would be wicked to stay with you. I will go, and you will forget me before I forget you!"

"You make a liar of me with such words! You stain my honor! I will always love you. And if you go, where will I find love? Where will I look for hope?"

"Do as I do: Trust in God and yourself. Believe in heaven. Hope to meet again there."

"Jane! Oh, my Jane! My hope, my love, my life!" Then came a deep, strong sob.

I had turned away. But, reader, I went back to him. I knelt down and turned his face to mine. I kissed his cheek and smoothed his hair with my hand.

"God bless you, my dear master!" I said. "God keep you from harm and wrong. Direct you, comfort you, reward you well for your past kindness to me."

A NEW LIFE

5

A new chapter in a novel is like the new scene of a play. When I pull the curtain, you must imagine me many miles away from Thornfield — for I left my master that very night.

I will not weary you, dear reader, with the story of what I endured. It is enough to say that kind people took me into their home and found me work as a school teacher. And did I forget my master? You do not know me very well if you could think that.

Weeks and months went by. He was always in my thoughts. And I was haunted by the fear that he might be dead. Finally, I wrote to Mrs. Fairfax for news of him, but two more months went by, and she did not answer my letter. I was torn with doubts. I did not know what to do with my life.

Should I remain where I was? Should I go, as one friend urged me, as a missionary to India? Should I go in search of Mr. Rochester and put my troubled mind at rest?

One night near midnight, I could not sleep. The room was full of moonlight. Deeply, sincerely, I prayed: "Show me the path I should take!" Suddenly, my heart began to pound. A strange feeling came over me. I trembled. And then from somewhere I heard a voice cry out: "Jane! Jane! Jane!"

"Oh, God!" I gasped. I knew the voice well. It was the person I loved best in the world — Edward Rochester! It spoke in pain and misery. It was a call for help.

"I am coming!" I cried. "Wait for me! Oh, I will come! Where are you?" I listened, but there was no answer.

I rose at dawn, packed a few clothes, and set out for Thornfield. Two days later I arrived. But where the great hall had stood was a great, black ruin. Around the burned remains was the silence of death. I had to know what had happened. I looked for the answers to my questions in the nearby town.

"Do you know Thornfield Hall?" I asked the innkeeper. "Is Mr. Rochester living there now?"

"No, ma'am," he said. "No one is living there. You must be a stranger. Last fall Thornfield burned to the ground."

"How did it happen?"

"There was some lady living there — a crazy lady. She turned out to be Mr. Edward's wife. Somehow she got away from her keeper, Mrs. Poole, and set fire to the house. Mr. Rochester was all alone. He had sent Mrs. Fairfax off, and the little girl he sent to school."

"But what about the fire?" I cried.

"Well, ma'am. I saw this myself. The woman — his wife — climbed on the roof. We saw him try to get her. We heard him call, 'Bertha!' But she jumped. She lay smashed on the rocks below — her blood and brains all over. It was terrible!" He shuddered. "Then, poor Mr. Edward — "

"Is he alive?" And I dreaded to hear the answer.

"Yes, ma'am, but he'd be better off dead, I think. You see, he's blind — and worse. He got trapped under a burning beam. It crushed his hand, and the doctor had to cut it off."

"Where is he? Where does he live now?"

"At Ferndean, a small farm he has about thirty miles from here. He lives there with a couple of servants."

Reader, it took me another day to reach Ferndean. I arrived just at dusk. As I neared the house, the front door opened. Slowly a man came out and stood on the step. It was my master, Edward Rochester.

His body looked the same except for the sleeve tucked into the front of his coat. It was in his face I saw the

difference. He looked like a wild, caged beast. But do you think I was afraid of him? No, reader. I loved him better than ever.

As I watched, a servant came out and led him back into the house. Quickly I went to the back door and knocked.

"Mary," I said to the woman who answered. "Do you know me?"

She jumped as though she had seen a ghost. "Is it really you, Miss Eyre? Have you come back to the master?" Before I could answer, a bell rang. "The master wants me, Miss," she said, filling a glass with water.

"Is that what he rang for?" I asked. "Give me the glass, Mary. I will take it to him."

My hand was shaking so hard I spilled half the water on my way to the parlor. The room was dark and gloomy. A small fire burned in the grate. And there stood my beloved master by the fireplace, his head bowed. Beside him lay Pilot, his old dog. When I came in, Pilot picked up his ears and began to whine. Edward turned his sightless eyes toward me.

"Give me the water, Mary," he said.

I went nearer and handed him the water, but Pilot followed. "Down Pilot!" I said.

Mr. Rochester stopped with the glass halfway to his lips. "Who is this?" he demanded. "Answer me! Speak again!"

"Will you have a little more water, sir? I spilled half of it," I said.

"Great God! What sweet madness is this!"

"No madness, sir. You are too strong for that."

He put out his hand, and I stopped it with mine.

"Her very fingers!" And he gathered me to him. "Jane Eyre! Jane Eyre!" was all he said.

"My dear master," I answered. "I have found you. I have come back to you."

"Is it my Jane? My living Jane?"

"You touch me. You hold me. I am not air, am I?"

"My darling! You are not a dream? I will not awake and find you gone?"

45

"I will never leave you — from this day on."

"You will stay with me? But, Jane, you can't! You are young. You must marry one day."

"I don't care about being married."

"You should care! If I were not blind and crippled, I would make you care."

"All my heart is yours, Edward. Would you send me away from you? We have always been friends."

"Ah, Jane. It is not a friend I want. I want a wife."

"Then choose, sir, her who loves you best."

"I will choose her I love best! Jane, will you marry me?"

"Yes, sir."

"Oh, my darling! God bless and reward you!"

"Edward, if ever I did a good deed in my life; if ever I thought a good thought; if ever I prayed a sincere prayer — I am rewarded now. To be your wife is, for me, to be as happy as I can be on earth."

And so, dear reader, my tale is nearly ended. It ends happily because God answered our prayers. That night — five days before — Edward, lonely and miserable, cried out to me: "Jane! Jane! Jane!" My heart heard his call for help, and I found him once more.

I married him. After two years, some sight came into his one eye. And when our first baby was put in his arms, he could see his son. We have been married ten years now, and I know what it is to live for — and with — what I love best on the earth. I have been blessed.

GLOSSARY

bigamy (big′ ə mē)   the act of marrying a person when already legally married to another person

conversation (kahn′ vər sā′ shən)   an informal talk between two or more people

governess (gəv′ ər nəs)   a woman who takes care of a child in a private home

missionary (mish′ ə ner′ ē)   a person who goes to another country to teach his or her religion

ward (wȯrd)   a person who is under the care or control of another person